In the Mountain's Shadow

By The Same Author

Razorblade

Fragmentations

In The Mountain's Shadow

Isabella Falconeri

Talon & Quill

This novel contains depictions of starvation, violence, child loss, psychological trauma, and survival in extreme circumstances, including scenes of abuse and more. Reader discretion is advised.

1

The Necklaces

In times of famine, the devil feeds on flies.

- GERMAN PROVERB

Her family, like other families, had no food to celebrate with.

They'd had very little for a very long time. In desperation, they'd taken to grinding bark between two stones and mixing it with water to make a paste for the children. Her grandchildren were ages three, nine, and thirteen.

The littlest one was the most demanding, always fighting for more than her siblings. She was adored by the whole family. Every whim was granted. The middle child was the adventurous one; he would disappear for hours and return with trinkets and small trophies from his explorations. The eldest was grim, silent, and would rarely leave his mother's side. He was a dutiful child who hadn't been spared many of the truths the younger ones had missed. He was a strong, dependable boy who gave better counsel than adults three times his age. The three children were bright stars in her life; there was nothing she wouldn't do for them.

Widespread poverty had left their family with nothing. They sold all they had, and worked whenever possible. It was difficult for her to get any work, anytime she presented herself to the wards for employment, she was turned down. "Too feeble" and "Too old" were often the reasons cited for rejection. She made many attempts, but the answer remained the same. While she was neither feeble nor, in her mind, very old; of the hundreds in line before her and after her, her age excluded her from selection.

She was a tinkerer by trade, given problems and able to find solutions. More often of the mechanical kind, but not always. She'd never been presented with a problem she couldn't solve… until now.

The last possessions she owned were the knobs from the dresser her late husband had made for her as a wedding present years past. She'd long ago lost her capacity for sentimental nonsense, but they were the last vestige of a bygone era where her children and her children's children didn't look up at her in malnourished despair.

None of the children had anything of their own, and she decided that the last item in her possession would be the first in theirs. Something for each of them to call their own. The melted-down metal was painstakingly transformed into three distinct necklaces. Each had a long chain and a thin rectangular pendant, hand-carved with the child's initials. She presented it to them on the eve of the new year. She'd never seen any of them so happy, it was the best day of her life.

A week later, the youngest child died.

The family buried the child in the backyard. There was no money for a proper burial.

The day before, the child had been acting strangely, and the family gathered whatever they could to send for a doctor.

Diagnosis: Malnutrition.

From that day forward the eldest was mute and the middle child no longer explored. One week later the doctor returned. A proposition. The family could stay with the doctor. They would be fed and cared for, provided they work. Only… not the old woman. The same refrain 'too old' and 'too feeble.'

Her daughter thought to decline, but the old woman wouldn't let her. The old woman decided to leave. She would do what needed to be done in order to ensure her family survived. One less mouth to feed. The daughter, knowing the offer might extend the lives of her two remaining children, acquiesced to the proposition.

The old woman, having made her decision to leave, puzzled over her next step. Where would she go? There was no place left unbroken. Populated areas tended to be dangerous and were breeding grounds for sickness.

There was no food. No money. No work.

It was her daughter who suggested the mountain.

The old woman hadn't thought of it, but it seemed like a welcome resting place.

Her decision made, she kissed the sleeping heads of her grandchildren, embraced her daughter, and left before dawn.

2

The Sacrifice

The old woman's name was Park, and she had been walking for a very long time.

She could see the mountain looming darkly above her. A monstrous form.

She walked in its shadow.

Every time she stumbled, every time she felt the severe pangs of hunger, she turned her thoughts towards her grandchildren. Thinking of them gave her mind a place to rest while her body pushed on.

Her first step inside the tree line at the base of the mountain felt heavier than all the others combined.

The forest canopy deepened the surrounding darkness.

She'd been told once that survival and death were choices. Choices a person made.

A person either allowed themselves to die… or they convinced themselves to survive. These words had long ago been given to her by her mother. Given at her father's gravesite. She remembered the feeling of her small hand in her mother's larger one. Her neck craned and her mother's face haloed by the rays of the inconsiderate sun behind her.

Park shivered, her memory translating the biting wind into the feeling of her mother's long fingers as they traced their way down her small cheeks, wiping away her tears.

Park's memory was a fickle thing. It failed her periodically. It was erratic, like the movements of a fly. This memory hit her heavily. Smell, touch, sight. All reality paled in the face of a simple moment between herself and her mother on a bright sunny day many years ago. Frozen in time for a few short seconds.

It was then that she saw it, the rising earth. The mountain's gate.

Here forest, there sky.

Here darkness, there light.

Here death, there life.

She thought about the decisions she'd made which had led her to this moment. Her single goal fulfilled. She had come here to die. To follow the natural instinct to ritualize her own death. In the most sacred way. Alone in the forest, under the swaying canopies. The breath of the earth swirling around her. Taking back what it had given so long ago. Assimilating herself into the great wide world.

Afterlife.

After. Life.

It seemed adequate. A good word. She rolled it around her tongue while she walked.

She'd originally meant to select a resting place just inside the tree line, but after pushing on for so long, she couldn't seem to stop herself. Her feet kept moving, her legs kept pumping. Neither the body nor the mind had made their decision to stop.

Not yet.

The Heart Is a Lonely Hunter… an ancient book she'd read long ago as a child. She neither remembered neither the content nor the author, but the title had stuck somewhere lodged deep within her subconscious for this very moment. It's funny the things your mind chooses to hold on to. And then, like an eager child, presents itself just at the right moment. So excited by its own ingenuity.

She yawned deeply.

Walking while dozing was a special skill she'd mastered over the years. Her stumbling cadence not changing much between flickering states of consciousness and unconsciousness.

Her step faltered once and she dropped to her knees on the spot, asleep in moments. Her dreams were filled with terrible things–the angry howling of wolves filled the air.

3

The Dead

When she finally woke, the world around her was blindingly bright. Her dry throat rattled in protest as she tried to move her stiff joints. In an attempt to orient herself, she thought back to her last hazy moments of consciousness.

She remembered the wolf cries in the nighttime and glanced around warily unsure if they'd been figments of her dreamlike hallucinations.

She was in a clearing. Nearby there was a scattering of discarded bones, some of which had remnants of rotted meat still clinging to them. Her hunger won out over her caution, and she felt herself lose control. Her weak body moving of its own volition. She fed ravenously on the remains. There wasn't much left, but it was more than she'd had in a long time.

She was sick almost as soon as the first few morsels hit her stomach. Unable to control her retching she began to sob. She cried for her lost family and her lost life. She cried for the things she'd never had. The loss of dignity and the absence of comfort. She cried for the people she'd survived and the people who would survive her. This was no place for humans.

Suffering wasn't meant to be permanent.

The old woman tried to reach the numbness… the place that allowed her to live as she had; to survive in hopes of better days.

She shook her head, clearing it of the weaving net of

despair. Whatever may happen, she didn't want to die in pain. She needed to leave this awful place, pain thrived here. She began to pick her way carefully across the shadowy glade. As she walked her feet sank a little deeper with each step… no, not a glade, a bog.

Looking down she saw a human hand, its gnawed fingers just breaking the surface of the muddy ichor. The fingers seemed to point at her in accusation. Horrified, she realized where her small meal had come from and, retching quietly again, she hurried away as fast as she could.

She ran faster and further than she had since she was a child. Trees and branches whipped past her, stinging her face and arms. She tripped and tumbled downwards. The fall was long, her momentum propelling her forward, she fainted, unconscious long before reaching the bottom.

She didn't regain consciousness until late afternoon the next day. Her hip was stiff, and moving her legs was a struggle. The tiny stinging pain was just another ache to add to the rest. Streaks of sunlight left a dusty brightness, just light enough for her to see by. As she stood, she noted her surroundings. She was in a small, overgrown garden. Her fall had broken the weak fence which protected it. The garden bordered an old cabin.

She shouted in happiness, it was the first time she had heard her voice since leaving her family.

She approached the cabin and tried the door. The hinges were rusty and unused. Heaving her small weight against it, it opened begrudgingly, inch by inch. When she peeked in, the only thing she could see in the pale triangle of light was the path of thick dust cleared from the entryway by the movement of the door. This place had been deserted for a very long time.

She squeezed through the space she'd made, barely able to breathe. Every inhale thousand swallowed particles, and every exhale, a whirlwind.

Covering her mouth with the sweat stained neck of her shirt, she walked to a dirty window, hoping to let in more light and fresh air. A leggy spider moved obligingly for her.

When the window finally gave, the fresh air blew in the scent of the forest, the wind making minute adjustments to everything it touched. She watched for a long time, breathing deeply, until the aching in her belly pulled her back from her reverie.

In the new colors painted by the open window, she saw the entirety of the sparsely furnished cabin. A fireplace, some cupboards, a small bed at the end of which was a large trunk, and a sturdy looking table.

She felt comforted by the shared loneliness of this place. She moved further into the room stepping softly. The small thud of her footsteps dampened by the thickness of the dust. She opened the cupboards one by one. Inside the first was an assortment of clay cookware. In the second she found some glasses and utensils. It was in the third she found the baskets. Woven baskets, each holding little stores of dried food.

As she began to eat, she sobbed. It had been so long since she'd tasted anything so good. Snot and tears mixed trails down her dirty face. One of the food cupboards had a hole chewed through the bottom, the basket inside had been destroyed by mice, nothing remaining of whatever bounty it once held… and the other contained what must have at some point been some sort of fruit or vegetable… now only mold. Her basket, however, held at least one month's worth of jerky; she could live another month, if she rationed carefully.

On the first day she found the food, on the second the water well. She was too weak to draw up the bucket, so she used a length of rope tied around one of the smaller clay pots to draw up some water. She washed herself carefully, paying special attention to her wounds. Her feet had turned black in some places. Blood blisters, wounds reopened again and again, caked dirt from the many miles she had traveled.

She spent endless hours staring at the water, playing with it like a curious scientist with mercury; poking and prodding.

She used one of the bedsheets to wrap her chest, hoping the small support would allow her bruised ribs, made worse by the fall, to heal more quickly. Over the next week, she slept and ate and drank; too lethargic to do much else. The food slowly helped her to regain her strength. The first week it was all she could do. It was as if her body had finally been able to release and let go. All of the tension, all of the fatigue. It finally asked back some of what it had given.

After that first week, she began cleaning out the cabin in earnest; she'd waited until she felt better to search the trunk. The red oak chest at the bottom of the bed. So large, so promising. Her past had taught her that good things come with heavy burdens.

4

The Hermit

When she finally got enough courage to open the chest, it revealed more than she could have possibly believed.

The cabin's last resident had kept a diary. In the diary were drawings, some were maps to nearby locations on the mountain where edible plants grew, drawings with distinguishing marks, noting which plants were poisonous and which weren't. Some entries were recipes; in the binding of one of the last books–she found a map. A map to a nearby creek. She carefully placed each of the journals back into the trunk, knowing these would be her salvation.

It wasn't until her second week, after another night of coughing the thick dust that she moved the bed in order to clean beneath more thoroughly. There she found the small hatch. She opened it, calling down quietly, afraid she might be answered.

She could barely see anything, only the small light which crept through the cracks in the floorboards. The thin rays allowed her to make out some of the shapes. The hatch led to a very small pantry, though nothing worth eating remained. She left the small cavern-like hole quickly, feeling unwelcome, and closed the hatch tightly when she exited; hoping to never need to return to that secretive coldness under the house again.

Her food supply ran low quickly. There hadn't been much of it to begin with. She knew she needed to search for more food. Taking care to pack lightly and using the journals as her guide, she began her first trek from the cabin.

She'd been frightened to leave the cabin for fear that it was only a dream. So frightened, in fact, that she had done only just out of sight and quickly returned many times before she could reassure herself that it would still be there upon her return.

When she reached the place marked on the map in the book, she found very few of the edible plants listed. As the day grew longer, she began to grow more and more desperate… knowing she had waited too long to search for food. She brought back her small bounty and hung it to dry as the book instructed.

From then onward, she went each day to a new

location described in the books, making notations in the margins, detailing what she found and how much and whether new growth meant a potentially bountiful trek at some future date. Each time she brought back a little, but barely enough. When the meat ran out, she felt herself weakening more quickly than before. It was like her body, once given bounty, could no longer function without.

On occasion she was able to trap small animals. The first time she attempted this, she sliced the pad of her thumb deeply. She knew the dangers of infection and though her other wounds had been healing nicely, there were a few scrapes that had reddened and she'd begun to worry.

Knowing she lacked medical training and hoping the books would help, she began reading through all the books in earnest. None of the books she read so far had anything that could help, but there was one book she had yet to read… the one which ended in blank pages. The journal which contained the map to the creek.

In this journal, she found some drawings of medicinal plants. She washed her thumb and bandaged it with a bit of cloth from her trousers. The next morning, she set out. This path was much more treacherous and took much longer than many of her other trips. She'd never before spent a whole night away from the cabin.

The trek hadn't started well, she'd slipped early on and nearly broken her ankle. She had to break through alder-like undergrowth and was stabbed by long thorns many times in the process. When it was time to make camp, she remembered the wolves and decided it was best to climb a tree. She was restless all night, ears tuned for any sound.

At dawn the next morning she heard them howling nearby. She shivered and spent the next few hours wide awake. In the early afternoon, she convinced herself to climb down. She hadn't heard the wolves in hours and she needed to get to the creek.

By late afternoon, the path ended at a steep hill and finally crested on a ledge. The creek was beautiful, sun sparkling in the rippling waves. She was surrounded by tall trees. She located the one drawn in the book, and prepared the bark in the manner described. After applying it and gathering more for home, she walked around the creek, searching for anything else she might find useful.

She knew it was growing far too late, but she felt something. An unfinished act. It was almost nighttime when she found it. The remains of an old woman, sitting at the base of a tree. The woman had died without violence, nestled comfortably in her resting place; and at the old woman's side, a familiar sight.

Reverently, she picked up the newest journal,

leafing through its pages. This one was not like the others, this one had whimsical characters drawn on every available space, musings about the mountain, poems written with a light hand. She placed the journal carefully onto the woman's lap.

The old woman had given Park an inheritance. Gifted her with life and shelter. She buried the stranger and her book, covering the gravesite with heavy stones, ensuring that nothing would ever disturb her from her resting place. When Park was done, she rested her hand lightly on top of the freshly disturbed earth, whispering an old poem she barely knew the words to.

She made her way back without incident.

5

The Routine

After a time she developed a routine.

She became familiar with the woods which surrounded her clearing and was able to make her way with relative ease. She was constantly threatened with starvation and constantly busy. Things broke, she fixed them. Things needed to grow, she planted them. She became apathetic to anything but her growing list of ‘things which needed to be done.’

Falling into the comfortable monotony of routine.

It was on the way back from the creek that it happened.

Nineteen times she'd made the trip, in almost as many months, before she actually saw them. The wolves. She'd become careless. When she saw them she knew they smelled her. She moved slowly and walked back to her campsite, making her way up into the tree and waited for two days.

She didn't see them again for another long while. She never forgot her lesson, though, and she was always careful and watchful. She'd lost count of how many times she'd been to the creek before the next time she encountered the wolves.

This time, they were not after her.

A man's screams tore through the dark underbrush. She was still weak now, but had developed wiry strength. She knew she was no match for the wolves, and it took her time to convince herself to try to help. In the end, knowing that someone was suffering a death she'd only barely escaped herself on more than one occasion, she made her way down her tree.

Gathering a thick branch, she wrapped some dry brush to the tip with cloth from her pack. She started a fire as quickly as she could and ran towards the screams. Torch blazing thickly in front of her.

When she found them, she stopped in terror. The scene was carnage and there were more of them than she remembered. She searched the furry hides for the source of the noise. Then she saw him. The man's eyes were wide, they looked black in the light of her torch. He reached for her beseechingly; screaming in pain. Her fear now quieted by his need, she began screaming at the wolves, brandishing her torch. They barely moved, snarling ferociously.

She stormed them to get closer to him.

The wolves separated, moving back a few paces, circling their prey. Their eyes glistening in the firelight; howling their anger. The man grabbed at her legs.

"Can you walk?" She hissed, barely audible over the noise of the wolves and the moaning of the man.

He pulled himself up to a sitting position, "I…I…I don't know," he sputtered.

There was blood pouring down his face and a flap of skin where a wolf had nearly accomplished scalping him.

"You will have to," she said, bracing herself, offering him a hand.

One of the wolves dove into the small clearing she'd made, angrily snapping at the man's toes.

He grabbed her hand with both of his and yanked himself up. As he stood, he doubled over clutching his stomach and moaning.

"Come on!" She snapped. He put an arm over her shoulder and they began hurriedly limping away.

She tried brandishing the torch every which way, but the wolves were hunting, and she couldn't keep track of all of them.

They hadn't gone far when one of the wolves attacked them from behind

They both fell over, the torch nearly snuffed out, she leapt back to her feet quickly, adrenaline pumping. The wolf was worrying at the man's shoulder, the man was screaming and trying to beat it away one-handed.

She hit the wolf with the torch and it whined; quickly disappearing back into the darkness of the forest. A smoldering glow remained where the fur on its face had been charred from the flame.

Another wolf appeared from the darkness on the other side of her. She could see its eyes, mingling with those of the others from the pack.

"We'll have to climb," she said.

She had him try to climb first; he could barely get himself up over the lowest branch. The stretching and pulling tore at his already damaged body. He sobbed and tried again.

She groaned inwardly. Knowing if she tried to help him, the wolves would attack, and if she went first, he would die.

"Well then, plan B, you'll have to manage walking by yourself. I can't keep us safe and help you walk at the same time."

He grunted in acknowledgment. Slumping he used the tree to keep himself steady. His first step, he stumbled, falling into the next tree. Using the trees to keep himself upright, he stumbled from one to the other, sobbing in pain.

She kept the wolves at bay as they went on. They moved slowly, so slowly. Her shouting directions at him if he strayed off course. The wolves kept pace, doubling back and snarling at one another when they broke formation.

After what felt like hours, the morning light began to grow slowly brighter as the torch grew dimmer. When they finally reached the cabin clearing, the man cried out in joy and began crawling towards the house.

When they were both inside and the door shut, she kneeled on the floor and sobbed. She had not believed they would make it, but now that they had, the wolves had been led right to her home.

She helped the man onto the bed. She took stock of his wounds. Not only was the man starved, but his wounds were grave. She gave him water and food.

When he saw the food he cried out. He kept asking for more, and by the time he was asleep, he had eaten everything in the house.

He slept in fits, screaming often. She tried to wash the wounds but he wouldn't let her, the pain too much. He died less than a week later.

The dead man was in her bed and the wolves were scratching at her door.

She had nothing left to eat in her house and she had lost a lot of energy getting the man back. As her adrenaline wore down, she was left exhausted and hungry. She couldn't leave the house. The wolves barricaded her in with their incessant howling. She sat at her table and stared at the dead man and cried. She had tried to save him only to end up killing herself in the process.

She thought of the old woman by the creek.

She stared at the dead man.

She thought of the people she had left behind.

She stared at the dead man.

She thought of all she had done until now to survive.

She stared at the dead man.

It took her less than a day to make her decision. She hated herself. She didn't want to. She warred with herself for hours. The wolves never ceasing their patrol outside.

She blamed the man for it.

She blamed him while she dressed and washed his body.

She blamed him while she cut.

She blamed him when she lit the fire in the fireplace.

She blamed him when her mouth began to water

and she blamed him when she took the first bite and

liked it.

After a week, the wolves left the cabin glade. For two weeks longer, she stayed close to the cabin, not straying too far and never leaving without a branch or her knife. The week after, she became bolder. She reset her traps and began foraging again for food. She traveled farther now.

Adding new information to the books.

It wasn't too soon after that she realized the wolves were stealing from her traps. She could no longer get new meat. Each time she set a trap, they would steal whatever she had caught before she could get to it. She had debated whether to continue setting the traps but considered that the more well-fed they were, the less likely they were to attack.

They knew where she lived and she could no longer keep anything edible outside. They'd destroyed her garden and eaten everything in it. She built a sturdier fence and replanted what she could. She knew she'd need to be able to find a new source of meat soon, and after some deliberation, she made a small net, stringing it high between two trees. From then on, the only meat she could catch and eat were birds. Too high in the trees for the wolves to steal.

It took a long time for the meat she had in the hatch below the house to run out, but when it finally did, she was worried. Eventually, she became thinner and weaker. The birds were too infrequent to maintain a healthy diet and the wolves were impossible to outwit. She knew they watched her, she'd seen them in the corners of her sight. She began to recognize the individuals.

One of them, a charcoal black one, was the smallest and least aggressive of the pack. He became more and more bold while the others lost interest and roamed elsewhere. This one she named Ripple. He had wide watery blue eyes which would ripple in the light every time he moved his head.

At first, she was wary, but soon she realized she might try to befriend him. She would leave him bits of food when he followed her. Tempting him with berries. She had never been closer than a few feet to the animal nor he near her, and they both remembered the natures of their companionship, knowing to tempt it had the potential to be fatal.

Eventually, the wolf began to lie asleep outside her door at night, and anytime anything came near, she was alerted instantly. The wolf would signal her with a small noise and she would awaken immediately. Ripple would always vanish after his initial warning, to either hunt or flee, depending on the size of the intruder. Whenever he caught anything, he would leave her a small parting gift, and in return, she left him as much food as she could spare.

The companionship was welcome. She spoke to the wolf often, rambling incoherently, the sound of her own voice more soothing to her than she realized.

She eventually devised a few new traps which were too far from the wolves' reach and was able to slowly restock her supplies.

6

The Deserter

One early morning she had just begun to pack for a trip when she heard Ripple tearing off into the thicket. Thinking he may have heard some small prey in the distance she disregarded it and continued to get ready. When she opened the front door, she was greeted by a pistol, pointed directly at her left eye.

Immobilized, she stared into the black bottomless circular hole. Her vision narrowed until it was swallowed by the gun's black maw. Shock and fear made her legs weaken. She hadn't yet registered the person holding it when laughter split the air. The sound was distorted, muffled by the thunder of blood rushing in her ears. The pistol began to tremble, the once-steady grip faltering. The arm sank, the chest heaved, and the knees buckled.

She still hadn't looked at his face.

This person, wearing the rags of what was once a military uniform — a deserter. This man, who had intruded on her abandonment. Her solitude had, until now, been a symptom of her survival. It had kept her alive and she had become so wrapped in its warmth and predictability that she had forgotten that the entire world outside her mountain teemed with humans doing much the same thing as she.

She had nearly forgotten the reason she had ventured into the mountain in the first place.

She had let herself forget, willingly, the comfort of people. Knowing that people, for her, most likely meant a death sentence.

People were no longer empathetic and helpful. They had, over time, grown more and more dangerous. This stranger was very dangerous.

She scrutinized him, now that the gun had been withdrawn from her face. She waited for his laughter to subside, not knowing how mad he was, or how mad she had become. Not knowing how long it would take him to kill her and take everything she had.

Slowly regaining his composure, he said, "old woman, take me inside and feed me." Not knowing his intentions and wondering if he planned to shoot her in the back, she didn't move. His smile faded quickly. Looking in his eyes, she saw watery blue, they reminded her of the wolf. The wolf, the runt, the predator. He hit her across her face with the butt of his pistol.

"Move aside," he said coldly, "I'll find the food myself."

The blow had moved her back from the doorway, the recoil moved her even farther away. He sauntered into the cabin. Looked over the things she had claimed and revived from their dusty deaths. After he surveyed the small cabin he nodded approvingly.

Glancing at her disdainfully, "food," he commanded menacingly.

She begrudgingly showed him the food in the cupboards, knowing he would find it anyway.

When he saw her stores of food, he shoved her aside and swallowed almost everything she had saved in a moment. Less than fifteen minutes later, the food had all been vomited back up on her floor. The outdoor heat cooked the smell into the floorboards.

Wiping his mouth raggedly, indicating the mess with

his pistol "clean it up," he croaked.

She began to cry. Nothing could be done about the food. She had spent months restoring her supplies and he'd laid waste to them in moments. Retching, she used an old rag to try to wash away the filth; she cleaned the mess as quickly as she could. Always keeping him in her peripheral vision. She kept envisioning him shooting her the moment her head turned away.

Drowning in the sense of sheer helplessness… the feeling of loss, she had a presentiment — everything she had built would be ruined by this horrible stranger.

She thought to herself, *if I die here, all the things I've done to keep myself alive will have been for nothing.*

He drank all the water in the cabin and told her to fetch more.

She left the cabin with the rag and tossed the retch into the woods where the wolves would find it. As she neared the tree line she began to run quickly, hoping she could reach it before he noticed. A shot whizzed past her head and hit the trunk of a tree not five meters in front of her.

"The water is to your left," he shouted hoarsely from the back window.

She went to the well and pulled up a bucket of fresh water. Her breathing ragged, she grabbed it and returned to the house. Her stomach clenched at the memory of the pistol striking her face. She put the bucket on the table, splashing some. Her fists clenching and unclenching.

He began rummaging through the trunk, throwing

the contents around as if they were trash. She uttered a small cry and moved involuntarily when one of the books, the books which had allowed her to learn how to survive on the mountain was tossed so violently that the spine bent backwards and pages spilled out.

"Please!" She choked.

He glanced at her with disdain and continued violently rifling. She hurried towards him, collecting the books and putting them aside where he may not do them any more damage.

He made a satisfied noise behind her, she looked quickly trying to discern the object of his pleasure.

Having found what he wanted, he stood slowly, facing away from her.

In his hands was a small length of rope. He began coiling it tightly around his first. He turned towards her and advanced menacingly. He grabbed her by the throat.

"Old woman," he said between gritted teeth, "you will feed me. You will work for me. You will do whatever I ask of you, and I will allow you to live. If you cross me, you will regret it."

She stared into his eyes, his ugly face disfigured by years of hateful despair. Tears collected in the corners of her eyes. He deftly tied the rope around her neck, "I'm going to sleep here," he said, indicating the bed, "and you will sleep outside."

She looked fearfully towards the door, dusk almost completed.

"Wolves," she hissed.

He looked at her strangely, considering. Her wiry body and her frail frame didn't disclose her strength.

He reconsidered, "the hearth, then," he said, nodding to himself. He tied the knots tightly and warned her before sleeping, "I sleep lightly."

Almost immediately upon laying on the bed, he was asleep, snoring. The last shreds of daylight slowly left their lingering shadows. She stared in his direction, eyes adjusting to the darkness. She was so frightened her hands shook as she grasped at the rope scraping roughly against her neck..

In her time, the time before the famine, she had seen people do terrible things to one another.

She reminded herself of the sins she'd committed to remain amongst the living. She thought about how much she was willing to give up to remain in this place she had made her home. This place which had welcomed her after she had given up everything else.

She had been lost before arriving here, a burnt out husk of her former self; and upon arriving she found something else left remaining in the ashes. She had deliberately given up her memories of other people, had intentionally left the misery and horror behind. She wasn't able to sustain them here, not with all the effort spent just existing. Moreover, she probably wouldn't be able to find her way off this mountain. She'd come to think of this place almost as purgatory.

A resting place.

A restful place to pause after all the hardships she'd experienced. A place which held her captive.

In her mind, this place wasn't malicious or benign. The mountain kept her safe, but the mountain required something of her in return. She was allowed to breathe and exist here but only if she denounced everything she used to know.

This place had laid claim to her and she to it. She belonged here and whether she wanted to or not, she could not leave… but she could fight.

Strengthening her resolve, she went to work quietly, trying to work the knots from around her neck. The rope scratched deeply and left bruises. With each tug she felt it constrict more tightly. She gave up on working the knots on her neck and tried to unravel the end tied to the fireplace. Her quiet tugging did nothing to loosen the knot. She fell asleep defeated, fingers cut and bleeding.

She awoke violently.

Her eyes flew open; she was face to face with him. He had pulled her up by her hair, the roots screaming in protest. Scrambling to get away from him, he screamed spittle in her face, "try to leave last night?" She shoved at him, hitting as hard as she could. He looked at the fresh wounds on her fingers and threw her against the wall in disgust.

"You have nowhere to go," he said, disgusted. "There's nothing left anywhere anymore." His eyes became clouded and lost, remembering. She had fallen to her hands and knees, she stared up at him, rage warring with fear. The gun was in his belt. She stared at it, willing it to fall into her arms. He looked at her looking at his gun.

He hit her again with the back of his fist.

He knelt down by the hearth and yanked her closer with the rope, giving himself some slack.

He then cut the knotted rope from the hearth with a knife he had taken from the kitchen. The sudden release of tension on the rope caused her to fall back and hit her head on the ground. He got up slowly, shoving her roughly with his foot.

"Water," he ordered.

She crawled away from him quickly towards the door. She saw a glimpse of her wolf disappearing into the forest edge as she left her cabin. Pain aching in each muscle she tiredly made her way towards the well knowing he was watching. She pulled up the heavy bucket from the depths of the well, straining tightly. She could only get a little bit of air through the tightened noose. She thought of asphyxiation and whether it happened slowly.

I could die like this, she thought to herself, *if it's easy, if it's slow.*

I could die like this.

She hauled the bucket back towards the house, thinking about what this place might become if it was left to the stranger.

He'd probably burn it to spite anyone else from living here, she thought sourly.

"I will protect this place," she promised.

Over the next few days she plotted, reading through the books for anything she could use. Every night she worried at the knots and every morning the rope was cut shorter. She knew that the stranger would kill her eventually.

His ravenous appetite never subsided. When the food ran out and there was nothing left of the stores she had saved, he beat her. She often crouched in corners when he was around, not wanting to attract attention and hoping that he continued to mistake her as weak and cowardly.

He forced her to take him on forays into the forest, noting which things she took, attempting to assimilate her knowledge so he could kill her when he felt comfortable fending for himself. She knew he watched, so she intentionally took food which was poisonous. The books were very clear which plants should be avoided, she studied them nightly.

She slowly began incorporating these poisonous plants more and more into the things she foraged. He never read the books; she suspected he couldn't read.

She felt secure in that he never allowed her much of anything she foraged.

She hoped that even though she was subjecting herself to the same poisons, the dosage would be so much less she wouldn't cause permanent damage. Or at least, she hoped, he would die first.

He never suspected her, even though he was often sick after eating. The weaker he became the meaner he got. The beatings grew more frequent.

For every bit of life she stole from him, he took just as much from her.

Her body changed in response to constant fear. Her sense of smell had become sharper. She could smell him advance on her, smell his moods.

Her reflexes had become faster.

She could dodge a blow simply by intuition. She could sense it, the moment before the blow, his cruel need to cause harm.

Sense it swell like a black tide.

A seed of hate grew more deeply rooted inside her. She would stare at him, imagining all the ways she would make him suffer. She was glad to be able to rid the mountain of such a monster.

After almost three months of enduring his near constant watchful eye, he began to slip. One day he left her alone in the house while he rummaged through the garden. She watched him leave, surprised at his oversight, and quickly slipped a small paring knife into her shoe. He came back almost immediately, nearly catching her in the act.

That night, when he finally went to sleep, she pulled the knife from her shoe.

It had moved during the day and sliced a deep gash in the bottom of her foot. She had been walking in a pool of blood for the latter part of the day.

She kept surreptitiously checking her steps to make sure she wasn't giving herself away with bloody footprints. As he started to snore, she took the knife out from where it was embedded, stifling a small cry. She cut herself free from the rope tether and quietly made her way to his side. Just as she lifted the blade to pass it across his throat, a cloud passed over the moon, throwing the room in complete darkness. She quickly stabbed downwards, catching a glimpse of his wide eyes just as the darkness came, only to go deaf as well as blind as a shot whizzed past her face.

Not being able to see or hear, she stabbed again and again, intent on her kill. He had moved after the first shot, the only thing her knife pierced were bedsheets. Trying to see through the night blindness, she swung the knife wildly.

Something cold hit the back of her head and she fell to the floor unconscious.

She woke to water being splashed on her face. She sputtered, her cheek lying flat on the table. She was sitting in her chair, but unable to move. Slowly regaining her wits, she realized she was tied down tightly. Her fingers splayed on the tabletop.

"Are you awake?" He asked, "I've been waiting for you."

She looked at him, her eyes straining upwards, her face immobile. She wondered how badly he would hurt her before he let her die. He flashed the knife she had used, letting it glint in the morning light.

She looked him over, checking him for injuries.

Have I managed to injure him at all? she thought despairingly.

Her vision cleared a little more and she saw an ugly, hastily bandaged wound running the length of his collarbone. From the color of the blood, she felt pleased she'd been able to wound him so deeply.

She hoped for infection, maybe she would still manage her task even after her death. She shook her head in disgust at her failure — she hadn't killed him herself, she felt pathetic.

He saw her looking at his wound. He chuckled lightly and, before she could react, he cut off the pinky and ring finger of her right hand. Her eyes went wide, she began to choke in surprise and pain, staring at her mutilated fingers in horror. A dizzying blackness overtook her.

Groggily returning to consciousness, she vaguely remembered screaming before passing out. She had hoped that she wouldn't give him the satisfaction of hearing her scream, but the fingers… her own flesh sitting in thick blood had been too much for her. The pain had been so immediate and terrible, but now all she felt was a horrifyingly cold ache. The fingers were still there, detached and undisturbed. Unable to cope with their loss, she stared at them dumbly.

She was in shock.

It was then she noticed him, sitting across the table, silently watching.

"I was going to make it even on the other side as well, for aesthetic purposes, you know," he said, musing.

He cleaned his fingernails with the blood streaked blade, "but I decided losing your capacity to grip would be worse for me in the long run, and I don't care to be burdened with carrying my own water."

He paused menacingly.

"Be careful you don't force me to reconsider," he said as he stood and left the table.

She remained tied to the table for five days. The only reason he didn't leave her longer was because the food ran out and he needed her to take him foraging. When he untied her, she couldn't move. She tried again and again to stand, but to no avail. The unimaginable ache in her bones left her rigid; it was as if she'd already succumbed to rigor mortis.

Impatiently he shoved her from the chair with his foot. Hitting the floor unlocked some of her muscles, but the pain was excruciating.

She cried out, feeling sorry for herself.

She saw his boots coming from around the table, she wouldn't allow herself to be weeping at his feet. She achingly pushed herself up to a crouch, audible pops could be heard, each feeling like a blow with a mallet.

She crawled to the well and began to wash herself. Her fingers had been glued together with dried blood, removing some of the dried blood made the wound reopen and begin to bleed again.

Weakly, she used some twine as a tourniquet and tied it tightly around the fingers awkwardly using her mouth and her good hand.

He looked on with detached interest. When she was done, they left to gather food.

He was whistling happily after they'd completed their forage and returned to the house. Even gregariously opening the door for her upon their return, affecting an overzealous, mocking bow.

Later, he gleefully cauterized the stumps; reveling in her renewed screams. The care of the wound almost as painful and cruel as the delivery of it.

Under supervision, she mused, *he might have been a good doctor.*

For a long while, there was never a moment, not a single instant, where he wasn't vigilant and cruel. Her hate for him grew, but there was nothing she could do. She had failed and now she felt powerless. Her body was weak and she fainted often, but was always awoken again by his swift kicks. She felt herself dying, but she was determined to make sure he died before she did. It took her many weeks to recover.

She imagined her retribution, the images playing over and over in her head, the stories she told herself before bed.

The poisons weren't working fast enough. She grew more and more frustrated. She watched his hands often, checking for tremors.

She made promises to herself.

She would hurt him.

She would maim him.

He would die a terrible death.

It took her months to find the exact plant she wanted. She'd gone through the pages of the journal trying to find something more potent. She'd read about it before but hadn't used it knowing if she ate any part of it, she would likely also die agonizingly.

Self preservation had restrained her before… but now, no longer.

The flower was blue, with veined leaves. She had never seen anything like it. She worried the toxic flower would harm her if she touched it bare handed so she used her shirt to wrap the buds she collected.

That night, she made him some tea.

She bade him drink it, meek in her stance. He eyed her warily. He gave her the cup and forced her to drink. He waited… and then waited some more. She tasted the brew, pretending to take a long draught and feigning reticence in giving it back.

Her fingers trembled.

The brew tasted like liquid fire running down her throat, burning holes inside her chest. Yet she stood resolute. She used that hate she'd cultivated so neatly to overcome the pain. The pain was nothing compared to the fire of her vengeance.

Finally satisfied, and seeing in her no outward change. He took his own deep draught and immediately gagged.

Gasping for breath he threw the cup at her, she dodged it, but it gave him time to unholster his gun. Wheezing, one hand on his throat, the whites of his eyes growing red as the blood vessels popped — he brought the gun up to aim.

As he fired, she charged, knocking him over the trunk. The first shot hit her shoulder. The second shot went wide. He was knocked unconscious in the fall, the gun tumbling to the side.

She grabbed it, took the butt of the gun and repeatedly hit him in the head with it until she was satisfied he wouldn't wake up for a long time.

When he finally did wake, he found himself tied to the chair exactly as she had been.

While he was unconscious, she had dragged him,

chair and all, deep in the woods and left him there.

The two parallel grooves dug deep in the soil leading her home.

Once she'd finished with him, she went to work creating a stew from healing herbs, an attempt at an antidote.

Her mouth bled, the inside raw. She was barely able to swallow the brew as her throat had swelled and was excruciating to move in any way.

Adrenaline gone, tasks done, she sat down, dozing fitfully.

Waiting.

Later that night the screams she'd been waiting for shattered the noisy silence of the forest. The howls of ravenous wolves enjoying their fill intertwined amongst the pained wailing.

She smiled to herself, blood caking her gums, and finally slept the deep, restorative sleep of the vindicated.

She didn't leave her house for a week. She swallowed the brew every hour and slowly regained her strength. Her voice never did recover though.

After she was well enough to walk, she went in search of her wolf. Throughout her miserable time with the deserter, she'd seen glimpses of the wolf, but he had never come near. She set out some of his favorite berries and waited.

A few days later he returned as if nothing had happened.

This time, though, she managed to leash him with a rope — she'd learned the knots the deserter had used. She chuckled to herself, using his knowledge to further her own path towards survival.

She tied Ripple to the house and began to feed him some of the same healing brew she'd made herself not long before.

A week later, she found the first dead wolf. Not long after, she found the rest. She built a single grave for all of them, including the remains of the deserter.

Only once she was sure she'd found all the bodies did she untie Ripple. His howl was more hoarse than it had been previously, but otherwise he was as fit as before.

In the meantime, she'd tried unsuccessfully to remove the bullet from her shoulder.

She never managed to get deep enough without

fainting.

So she cleaned the wound and left it buried. She kept her arm in a sling.

It took two months to heal. Afterwards, she'd developed a tendency to, whenever lost in thought, probe the back of her shoulder, fingers feeling under the skin for the small lump she knew was there, the foreign body.

Before she had dragged the deserter into the forest, she'd taken his gun, his belt, and his boots. She stuffed leaves in the toes to fit them to her small feet. She loaded the gun with the last of the ammunition, tied the belt around her waist, her knife and his gun carefully holstered.

From that day forward, she never went anywhere without them.

It took her a long time to replenish her meager stock. She began using the cellar to store her food.

As a precaution, she left a small amount of food in the cupboards. This, she mixed with the blue flower. Anyone who ate from there would suffer a similar fate as the deserter.

7

The Family

Except for the slow turning of the seasons, there was nothing to disturb her routine.

She woke in the morning. Washed, cleaned, stared into the wilderness. She continued to fill the journals with useful information. She tested new plants. A thoroughly lengthy affair.

First, separate roots, stems, leaves, flowers.

Then rub on the inside of the wrist.

When no sign of irritation occurs,

boil a small portion and hold it to your lips.

Put it in your mouth and wait.

And lastly,

swallow.

Her wrist developed an acute sensitivity to toxins. After a while, she became adept at sensing when things were inedible. Her stomach became overly sensitive. She learned more and more about her environment. Writing down each new kernel of knowledge.

She explored further and further. Keeping logs of where she'd been. Whether there was anything edible and how to get there.

It was inevitable, really… when it finally happened.

Late one evening, before dusk, she stumbled onto a small family making their way into the wilderness.

It took her a full moment of shock before she turned and ran back the way she came, back into the darkness.

A voice hailed her from the clearing.

A mother and her two children, an older boy and a young girl. Park went over everything she'd seen in those first few seconds. The family was definitely starving. They seemed to be unarmed and they were overburdened with things.

She raged within herself.

Return? Or leave?

The voice called again.

"Please don't hurt us!"

She considered.

Taking a deep breath, knowing it was stupid, she returned silently, peering into the clearing from the comforting cover of the woods.

The mother stood, circling. The little girl huddled close to her, the boy glared into the encroaching darkness.

Park reappeared in the clearing. The mother gasped and gathered herself behind the boy. The boy scoffed at her:

"Mother! It's only an old woman!"

The mother peered out from behind her son, her eyes lighting up. The family advanced on Park quickly.

The old woman chose that moment to reveal her gun.

In tandem, all three cowered at the sight. The mother spoke, "my children and I are trying to find our way out. To the other side of the mountain. Do you know how to get there?"

Park shook her head No.

The mother shuddered, "we came through from the… the east, I think. I… I don't know. It was morning, it was still dark. We were in the mountain's shadow. We've been walking so long," she sputtered.

Park pointed to the West, indicating the direction opposite their entrance. Park then slowly untied a bag from her belt–everything she had spent the last few days foraging–and dropped it on the ground, looking at them pointedly. She took a couple steps back as she saw the mad hunger in their eyes.

Then, her fear winning out, she turned on her heel and ran.

She didn't return to her cabin for a week. Worried about leading them back to her home. She avoided many of her usual foraging grounds and hid in a hollow tree, surviving off of a cache of food and drink she'd hidden there long ago.

The sun rose in the East, she mused, it had been morning — they entered from the East. She thinks about the past, remembering. She entered from the West. The West is where she had come from; where her family still remained. She felt a pang in her chest. It had been so long, there was little possibility she'd be able to find her way back to them.

There was nothing she could do for her family anymore, but for this family… she could help.

She warred with herself. She could sense their menace when they thought she was a harmless old woman.

They would have killed her and taken everything she had.

She scolded herself.

You can't know that for certain, she rationalized, *you've become heartless in your old age.*

Guilt won out over caution, after that first week had passed, she resolved to find them again, to help in any way she could.

Perhaps, she thought to herself, *I shall watch them from afar at first, all I am obliged to do is ensure they make it out alive* and then, her conscience clear, she could return back to her home.

She had no idea how to track, but she managed to find the clearing she'd left them in.

From there she slowly made wider and wider circles outwards.

Her determination never faltered; her guilt at leaving them potentially defenseless weighed heavily upon her.

It took weeks to find them. They hadn't traveled in the direction she pointed. They had tried to follow her, but had gotten lost.

At her first sight of them, she saw only the mother and son. They were crowded around a small fire with some not-so-fresh meat.

She heard them whispering, too hard to tell what they were saying over the crackling fire. Their mouths munched robotically round, staring vacantly into the fire.

Like cattle–vacuous and empty, animalistic.

Staring.

Black eyes lit by dark flames.

There were no tears.

No remorse. Ruthlessness.

Park walked backwards slowly. Hand over mouth. A twig snapped. Both their heads lifted in unison, facing the sound.

Can she judge?

Has she not shared their fate?

Could she have prevented this?

But … their own family.

A child.

Park closed her eyes.

Never family.

Family is the most important thing in the world. What corruption would make a human place their own survival over that of a family member.

Unforgivable.

As a young child Park's mother had taken her to a church and on one of the stained glass windows there had been an image of a man in a desert next to a pile of bones; his dog. The man poised forever in teary-eyed supplication. She was too young to read and when she asked her mother to translate she was told it read something like, 'only after basic needs are met comes the return of sentiment.'

When she asked her mother for further clarification she was told: until thirst is quenched and hunger is fed, a human is nothing more than a husk of need; only upon satisfaction may fear, love, or regret return.

I didn't agree with it then, Park thought, *and I don't agree with it now.*

She unholstered her gun, entered the clearing and shot them both dead before they could react.

She took a log from the fire and burnt both the bodies.

She turned away slowly and walked home.

She never returned to that side of the mountain.

8

The Rabid

It was many years before she saw another human. Safe in the isolation and comfort of the mountain.

Ripple had long since died of old age.

When Ripple died, she lost her early warning system.

Without the wolf she became even more wary. She wanted another wolf, but she wouldn't put herself in danger to acquire one. She had claimed her part of the woods as her own territory after the pack had been poisoned, and no predators had dared challenge her since.

Her routine went uninterrupted for so long she forgot what having a companion felt like. She wasn't even lonely. It had been long since she'd wanted for anything.

Until, once again, her solitude was broken by the outside pushing in.

It was the middle of the night. Park did not sleep deeply anymore. She woke the moment she heard something in the woods.

The sound was like nothing she had heard before.

It reverberated through the trees.

She tore off the covers, remade the bed as quickly as she could, obscuring her presence, then slipped beneath it and into the cellar.

The door burst open minutes later.

Next time, I'll invest in building a lock. Who knew you'd need such a thing in the middle of nowhere, she thought wryly.

A frantic woman stumbled in, her clothes torn, her hair wild.

She darted to a cupboard in the kitchen and shut herself inside. Park could hear her weeping, her sobs loud despite her attempts at silence.

A shout rang out from the woods. It reminded Park of the sounds the wolves made when they neared their kill.

Both women heard it.

The cupboard woman went still.

Park might've imagined it, but she felt she could hear both their heartbeats hammering erratically, beating in time.

Then the door slammed open again, wrenched from its hinges.

Goddamit! Park thought.

Four men stormed in, tearing the place apart. They find the cupboard woman quickly. Her screams filled the cottage as they dragged her out.

She clawed at the cupboard frame, kicking like a wild animal. A boot stamped on her hand; she howled. A fist silenced her with a crack.

Park watched.

She had only three bullets.

There are four of them.

But she has other weapons.

This will not happen in my house.

The men threw the woman onto the bed. The frame groaned above Park. Three clambered on top while the fourth kept sentry.

Park, not pausing to deliberate, raised the cellar door a few inches, braced herself on the steps.

Breathing slowly, she aimed the gun at the one standing watch.

She fired.

Hitting him square in the chest.

A burst of a thousand bright red flecks sprayed forward and back as he tipped, mouth open in shock.

Bam.

He hit the ground, his unseeing eyes fixed on Park.

The men scrambled off the bed hollering.

They closed ranks around the fallen one and Park fired twice more.

One.

Two.

They crumpled, light gone dark.

The last turned to run—when the cupboard woman leapt from the bed onto his back, screaming like a banshee.

She tore at him with her nails. She grabbed the lower half of his jaw with one hand and wrenched

His scream broke into a crack as his jaw dislocated. He slammed her against the wall. Her grip slipped. She fell. He drove his boot into her stomach.

Park slid from beneath the bed, rope in hand.

While he was distracted, she slipped behind him and looped it around his neck.

A primitive garrote.

She twisted it around her arms for leverage.

Cinching it tighter and tighter.

He clawed at it desperately, his fingernails piercing his own flesh.

The cupboard woman looked up, her teeth bared. Bruising colored her beautiful features.

Seeing the man debilitated, she grabbed the knife from Park's belt, and bolted out the door.

Park was taken aback.

Where the hell is she going? Park thought. Then shook her head. *There goes the knife.*

Her attention snapped back to the man. Startled by the woman's flight, she had loosened her grip, giving him air.

He gasped.

Well shit, now I've got to start all over again.

He was weaker now, though, and stopped struggling sooner than she expected. When she was sure he was out cold, she laid him down.

She reached for the heavy trunk, dragged it over, hefted it—aiming by feel—and dropped it neatly onto his head, crushing it.

The skull gave way.

Blood spurted.

She sighed.

Better do the others too. Just to be sure.

When she had finished, she surveyed the wreckage.

Now I'll have to clean this mess, she thought.

She stepped outside cautiously, listening.

A low grunt drew her to the trees.

There she found her.

The woman tracked down the final man.

Astride his back, she had stabbed him so many times he was more hole than flesh.

His twitching legs the only sign of life

Merely moving with the force of each blow.

The only noise the soft grunts of effort, the squelch of flesh.

At the sound of Park's approach, the woman

turned, snake-like, knife raised.

Recognition dawned.

Her breath shuddered out; the knife lowered.

Tears streamed down her face.

"Thank you," she whispered.

Something unspoken passed between them. They buried the bodies together, scavenging whatever weapons they could.

They trekked to the river and washed themselves, removing the carnage.

From that day forward the woman became her shadow.

She learnt everything.

Helped wherever she could.

She even taught Park to track and meat became plentiful.

The two women worked together.

They survived together.

9

The Cohabitation

Not having truly lived with anyone for years, there is a period of change and adjustment for the old woman.

The younger woke up many nights screaming and wouldn't fall back asleep until she'd reassured herself the old woman was nearby.

The old woman recognized traits in the younger, similar to her daughter in certain mannerisms.

The way she stamped her foot in frustration when she didn't learn something as quickly as she'd like. The way she slid her fingers through her hair when she was deep in thought.

It reminded the old woman of her family.

On lone treks sometimes she shed a few tears, as many as she would allow herself, thinking about the past and the things she gave up.

She wondered about her daughter and her grandchildren.

She remembered their small fingers wrapped around hers. Their adoration. The way they smelled. Their soft skin brushing hers. She remembered the looks of joy the day they received her gifts, the necklaces.

One day, while lost in thought she slipped on a muddy

incline and fell down a steep ravine. At the bottom, barely conscious, she could feel each old wound as if it were new again.

Cursing herself for her stupidity she fell into the deep comfort of unconsciousness.

The younger woman found her a day later. In a panic she had been scouring the woods the moment she realized Park's abnormally long absence.

The younger woman built a handmade stretcher and brought the old woman back to the cottage.

It was a long, arduous trek. She had to stop many times.

Weeks passed while the younger nursed the old. Park began to depend on the younger as much as the younger depended on her.

They were safe together, they protected one another.

10

The Chain

Park aged.

She was less able to care for herself and unable to assist the younger woman in many daily tasks. After many years of quiet companionship and general contentment, she began to feel practically useless.

Her body not functioning as it should.

Park feared–with a presentiment common only to those past a certain age–the younger may be left alone soon.

She became what she was defined as: old… feeble.

She didn't want to become a burden to her adopted daughter. She considered her options.

She might wander away by the creek as her predecessor had done. But she knew the younger would be sad at her passing, so she delayed a little.

Not yet, she thought often.

Though her body had suffered much damage, and her mind believed it could command more than her flesh can answer, she still felt sharp.

Her thoughts raced, though her gnarled, pained fingers did not.

She would think to herself, *move faster, bend, get up.*

All manner of things she never once thought twice about.

But every single thing harder than before.

The disconnect between what she thought she'd be able to

do and what she was actually able to do was stark.

It was a dissociation of sorts.

Your mind thinking 'grab that', and moving onto the next thing, but your hand still slowly reaching, trembling as it hovered.

Almost like you have to slow your mind to match your body, rather than your body hurrying up to match your mind.

A painful prison.

A tender, fragile prison.

A gift worn bare.

It was a miracle to her that she had even lasted this long.

Lasted, she thought, *what a nonsense way of thinking about it, like the shelf life of an herb.*

She felt she would be ready soon.

One day, while she prepped the vegetables in the cabin, she sent the younger woman to gather more.

A while later–thinking she heard something in the garden–she was about to call out.

When another noise interrupted.

A quiet struggle...grunting.

She ran to the door. It began to open as she reached it.

Moving more stealthily than usual, she slid to the side quickly–her body obscured by the door–hidden from the intruder.

A young man–or rather the back of one–dragged the younger woman behind him like a doll.

The younger's head lolled, a gash ran down her temple to her chin.

The old woman saw red.

She shoved the door closed and leapt onto the man.

They struggled.

She was not as strong as she used to be, but her ire made her dangerous.

He thrashed and managed to grab hold of her right arm, wrenching it painfully.

It dislocated at the shoulder.

She screamed silently, and using her teeth, bit deeply into the soft flesh just below his ear…tearing.

Rending skin.

Jugular.

Hot blood spurted into her mouth and onto her face.

He threw her off.

She landed heavily on the table, breaking two ribs.

Hand held to his neck to staunch the bleeding, he roared.

Using the counter to brace himself, he kicked the table so it screeched to the other end of the room, pushing her away from him.

Park slid off into a heap on the floor.

His eyes fluttered as he sank to his knees.

Blood drenching his shirt.

"You hag," he whispered spitefully, "you awful hag! You've killed me!"

His blood colors the floorboards around him.

Park drags herself to the younger woman.

Checking on her.

Thankfully, the younger's eyes open, blinking slowly up at Park.

Park hugs her tightly. Bony fingers sinking into soft skin. Her breath hitches when the woman squeezes back, her ribs protesting

The death rattle of the intruder echoes through the cabin.

The old woman shudders.

Adrenaline gone, the shudder creates a map of sharp pains all throughout her body, so excruciating, Park nearly faints.

The younger woman lifts Park up and they stagger towards the intruder, leaning heavily on each other.

The old woman checks his pulse.

A chain brushes her fingers.

Curious, she pulls it out.

Upon seeing the pendant, her wail, the first sound she's made in decades shatters the peace of the glade.

A flock of birds shoot up into the sky, startled.

Thank You for Reading

Stories don't end on the page — they echo in the quiet places they leave behind.

In the Mountain's Shadow was born of questions: what we endure, what we sacrifice, and the fragile threads that bind us to one another.

If these pages moved you, I would be honored if you shared a brief review on Amazon or Goodreads. Your words help others find their way here — and help keep this story alive.

Until we meet again, in the spaces between stories

— Isabella Falconeri

Made in United States
Cleveland, OH
17 November 2025

26112391R00066